The Table, the Donkey and the Stick

Adapted from a retelling by the Brothers Grimm

PAUL GALDONE

McGraw-Hill Book Company

New York St. Louis San Francisco Auckland Düsseldorf
Johannesburg Mexico Montreal Kuala Lumpur
London Panama São Paulo Paris New Delhi
Singapore Sydney Tokyo Toronto

For Jean

Library of Congress Cataloging in Publication Data

Galdone, Paul.
    The table, the donkey, and the stick.

    SUMMARY: Three brothers who leave home because
of a greedy goat, return to share with their father
the magic rewards of their hard work.
    [1. Fairy tales.   2. Folklore — Germany]
I. Grimm, Jakob Ludwig Karl, 1785-1863. Das tap-
fere Schneiderlein.   II. Title.
PZ8.G127Tal   398.2   76-15559
ISBN 0-07-022700-4
ISBN 0-07-022701-2 lib. bdg.

1234567 RABP 789876

There once was a tailor who had three sons and one goat. As the goat nourished them all with her milk, she had to be well fed, and so she was led out to graze every day. This the three sons did in turn. One day the eldest took the goat to the churchyard where the greenest grasses grew, so that she might eat her fill and gambol about.

When it came time to go home he asked, "Well, goat, have you had enough?"

The goat answered:

> "I am so full
> I cannot pull
> Another blade of grass—meh-eh-eh-ehh!"

"Then come home," the eldest son said, and he led her to her stall and tied her up.

"Now," said the tailor, "has the goat had her proper food?"

"Oh, yes," answered the son, "she is so full she no more can pull."

But the father, wishing to see for himself, went out to the stall, stroked her, and said, "My dear goat, are you full?"

And the goat answered,

"How can I be full?
There was nothing to pull,
Though I looked all about me—meh-eh-eh-ehh!"

"What is this I hear?" cried the tailor. And he called out to his eldest son, "O, you liar, to say that the goat was full when she has been hungry all the time!" And in his anger he took up his yardstick and drove him out of the house with many blows.

The next day came the second son's turn. He found a fine place in the garden hedge where there were good green sprouts for the goat to enjoy.

Towards evening when he led her home he asked, "Well, goat, have you had enough?"

The goat answered:

> "I am so full,
> I cannot pull
> Another blade of grass—meh-eh-eh-ehh!"

"Then come home," said he and led her home and tied her up.

"Now," said the old tailor, "has the goat had her proper food?"

"Oh, yes," answered the son, "she is so full she no more can pull."

But the tailor went out to the stall and said, "My dear goat, are you really full?"

And the goat answered:
"How can I be full?
There was nothing to pull
Though I looked all about me—meh-eh-eh-ehh!"

"That good-for-nothing rascal," cried the tailor, "to let the dear creature go hungry!" And he chased his second son out of the house with his yardstick.

The next day the third son took her out. He found some shrubs with the tenderest shoots possible and left the goat to eat them.

In the evening when he came to lead her home he asked, "Well, goat, are you full?"

The goat answered:

> "I am so full,
> I cannot pull
> Another blade of grass—meh-eh-eh-ehh!"

"Then come home," said the third son. And he took her to her stall and fastened her up.

"Now," asked the old tailor, "has the goat had her proper food?"

"Oh, yes," answered the son, "she is so full, she no more can pull."

But the tailor, not trusting him, went to the stall and said, "My dear goat, are you really full?"

The wicked goat answered:

> *"How can I be full?*
> *There was nothing to pull,*
> *Though I looked all about me—meh-eh-eh-ehh!"*

"Oh, the wretches!" cried the tailor. "The one is as good-for-nothing and careless as the other." And he thrashed his third son's back with his yardstick till he ran away.

So the old tailor was left alone with the goat. The next day he went out to the goat saying, "Come, dear creature, I will lead you myself to the willows."

As he took her to the green hedges where there was plenty of food to her taste he said to her, "Now, for once you can eat to your heart's content."

He left her there until evening. When he returned and asked, "Well, goat, are you full?"

She answered:

> *"I am so full,*
> *I could not pull*
> *Another blade of grass—meh-eh-eh-ehh!"*

"Then come home," said the tailor. And leading her to the stall, he tied her up.

As he was leaving he turned and said, "Now then, for once you are full."

But the goat cried:

> *"How can I be full?*
> *There was nothing to pull,*
> *Though I looked all about me—meh-eh-eh-ehh!"*

When the tailor heard this he at once realized that his three sons had been punished and sent away unjustly.

"You ungrateful creature!" cried he, "I will teach you to show your face again among honorable tailors!"

He grabbed his yardstick and in a fury drove her away over the hill, and to this day no one knows where she ran.

The tailor felt very sad as he sat alone in his house. He would have been happy to have his sons back again, but no one knew where they had gone.

The eldest son became a carpenter's apprentice. He worked hard and when the time came for him to leave, his master gave him a little table. It wasn't much to look at, but when anyone set it down and said, "Table be covered!" instantly the little table was decked with a cloth and dishes with a roast and boiled meats and red sparkling wine to cheer the heart.

"Now I am set up for life," said the young carpenter and went merrily out into the world. When he was hungry, no matter where he was, he set down his table and said, "Table be covered!" and at once there was all the good food he could eat.

One day he thought he would go back to his father. Perhaps because of his wonderful table, he might be welcomed home.

On an evening during his journey home he came to an inn that was crowded with guests. They invited him to sit down with them and share their supper.

"No," said the young carpenter. "Please be *my* guests, instead."

They laughed and thought he must be joking as he put his little wooden table in the middle of the room and said, "Table be covered!"

At once it was piled with food much better than the innkeeper had provided.

"Eat, good friends!" said the carpenter. The guests were astounded but needed no urging. They took up knife and fork and fell to eagerly. What was most wonderful was that when a dish was empty, it filled right up again.

All this time the innkeeper stood watching all that went on. "Such cooking as this," he thought, "would make my inn prosper."

At last, late at night, they all went to sleep after the merry feast. When he went up to bed, the young carpenter left his wishing table standing against the wall.

The innkeeper, however, could not sleep. He kept thinking of the table and he remembered that he had in his attic a table very much like it.

So he fetched it, carried away the carpenter's, and left the other in its place. The next morning the carpenter paid his bill, took up the table, and went on his way, unaware that he was carrying off the wrong one.

When he reached home, his father received him with great joy. "Now, my dear son, what have you learned?" he asked.

"I have learned to be a carpenter," he answered.

"That is a good trade," said the father. "But what have you brought back with you from your travels?"

"The best thing I've got, father, is this table," said he.

The tailor examined it on all sides and said, "You have certainly produced no masterpiece. It is just a shabby old table."

"Ah, but it is a very wonderful one," replied the son. "When I set it down and tell it to be covered, at once the finest food and drink appear on it. Let us invite all our neighbors for a feast. The table will provide enough for all."

When the neighbors had gathered, he put his table in the middle of the room and said, "Table be covered!" But the table never stirred. When the poor carpenter saw that it remained empty, he felt like a fool.

The guests laughed at him and left as hungry as they had come. The father then returned to his tailoring and the son went to work for another master.

The second son apprenticed himself to a miller and when his time was up, his master said to him, "As you have behaved yourself so well, I will give you a remarkable donkey. He will pull no cart and carry no sack."

"What good is he then?" asked the young apprentice.

"He coughs out gold," answered the miller. "If you spread a cloth before him and say, 'Bricklebrit,' out come gold pieces."

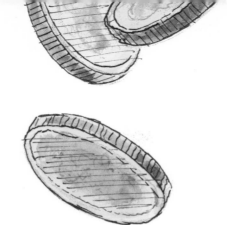

"That is wonderful!" said the apprentice and thanking his master he went out into the world.

Whenever he wanted gold he had only to say "Bricklebrit" to his donkey and there was a shower of gold pieces. He lived in comfort as his purse was always full. After he had been wandering about the the world for a long time, he thought he would go home to his father who would perhaps receive him kindly because of his gold-donkey.

And it happened that he came to stop at the same inn where his brother's table had been exchanged.

He was leading his donkey, and as the innkeeper was about to take it away to tie it up the young man said, "Don't trouble yourself. I will lead him to the stable myself, then I shall know where to find him."

The innkeeper thought that someone who was accustomed to looking after his own donkey could not have much money to spend. But when the stranger took two gold pieces from his pocket and told him to get him something good for supper, the innkeeper ran and brought him the best meal he could provide.

After supper the guest asked for his bill and the innkeeper, wanting to make all the profit he could, said that it would amount to two gold pieces more. The apprentice felt in his pocket.

"Wait a moment, innkeeper," said he, "I will go and fetch some more money," and he left the room carrying the tablecloth with him.

The curious innkeeper slipped after him. The guest had shut the stable door, so he peeped in through a knothole. He saw the stranger spreading the cloth before the donkey saying "Bricklebrit," and the donkey then coughed out gold, which rained upon the cloth.

"By thunder!" said the innkeeper to himself. "That is an easy way to get money."

The guest paid his bill and went to bed. But the innkeeper stole down to the stable in the middle of the night and led the donkey away after tying another donkey in its place.

The next morning the apprentice started out with the donkey, never doubting that it was his own. By noon he came to his father who was happy to see him again.

"What trade have you taken up, my son?" asked the father.

"I am a miller, dear father," answered he.

"What have you brought home from your travels?"

"Nothing but a donkey," answered the son.

"A donkey!" said the father. "You had much better brought me a nice goat!"

"But this is no common donkey. When I say 'Bricklebrit!' the good creature coughs out a whole clothful of gold pieces. Let us call all the neighbors together. I will make rich people of them all."

"That will be fine!" exclaimed the tailor, "then I need labor no more!" And he rushed out to invite the neighbors. As soon as they were all assembled around the donkey, the second son spread a cloth before him.

"Bricklebrit!" he cried. But no gold pieces came. The animal was no more unusual than any other donkey.

The poor young man made a long face when he saw that he had been taken in and begged pardon of the neighbors, who all went home as poor as they had come. The old man took to his needle once more and his son went to work for a miller again.

The third son apprenticed himself to a woodcarver. His brothers sent him word of how badly things had gone with them and how on the last night of their travels the innkeeper cheated them of their treasures. When the young carver had learned his trade and was ready to leave, his master, to reward him for his good work, gave him a sack with a stick in it.

"The sack may be very useful to me," said the young man. "But what is the good of the stick?"

"I will tell you," answered the master. "If any rascals do you any harm and you say, 'Stick, out of the sack!' the stick will jump out and beat them so soundly that they will hardly be able to move and it will not stop until you say, 'Stick into the sack!'"

The young man thanked him, took up the sack, and started on his travels. When anyone attacked him he would say, "Stick out of the sack!" and out jumped the stick to deal a shower of blows which quickly ended any threat.

One evening he reached the inn where his two brothers had been taken in and sat down to chat with the guests about the wonders they had seen in the world.

"Yes," said he, "you may talk of your self-spreading table and your gold-heaping donkey, very good things, but they are nothing in comparison to the treasure that I have acquired and carry with me in this sack!"

Then the innkeeper pricked up his ears.

"What in the world can it be?" thought he. "Very likely the sack is full of precious stones. And I have a perfect right to it. Don't all good things come in threes?"

When bedtime came, the third son stretched himself on a bench with the sack under his head as a pillow. The innkeeper, when he thought the young man was sound asleep, gently pulled at the sack to sneak another in its place. The woodcarver had only been waiting for this to happen.

As the innkeeper was giving a last quick tug he cried, "Stick, out of the sack!" Out flew the stick and at once began to beat the innkeeper's back. He begged for mercy! The louder he cried, the harder the stick beat him, until he fell to the ground, exhausted.

Then the third son said, "Give me the table and the donkey right now or this game will start all over again."

"No, no!" cried the innkeeper. "I will gladly give everything back if you will only make this terrible goblin go back into the sack."

"This time I will be merciful," said the young man, "but beware."
He cried "Stick, into the sack!" and the stick left him in peace.

Next morning the third son set out with the table and the donkey on his way home to his father. The tailor was glad indeed to see him again and asked him what he had learned since he had left home.

"My dear father," answered he, "I am now a woodcarver."

"A very skilled handicraft," said the father. "And what have you brought back with you from your travels?"

"A very valuable thing, dear father, a stick in a sack."

"What!" cried the father, "a stick! You can cut one from any tree!"

"But it is not a common stick, dear father. When I say 'Stick, out of the sack!' out jumps the stick upon anyone who tries to harm me and does not leave off till he is beaten and asks for pardon. Just look here, with this stick I have recovered the table and the donkey which the thieving innkeeper took from my two brothers! Now we must send for both of them and all the neighbors, too. They shall eat and drink to their hearts' content and we will fill their pockets with gold."

The old tailor could not quite believe all this, nevertheless, he called his sons and all the neighbors together.

Then the woodcarver brought in the donkey, opened a cloth before him, and said to his brother, "Now my dear brother, speak to him."

And the miller said, "Bricklebrit!" and at once so many gold pieces covered the cloth that they all had more than they could carry away.

Then the woodcarver set down the table and said, "Now, dear brother, speak to it."

As soon as the carpenter said, "Table be covered!" it was covered and set forth plentifully with the richest dishes. Then they all held such a feast as never before and remained through the night, merry and content.

And so—after that, the tailor put away
his needle and thread, his yardstick and iron,
and lived ever after with his three sons
in joy and contentment.

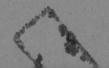